This book belongs to:

D1335972

First published 2016 by Walker Entertainment, an imprint of Walker Books Ltd
87 Vauxhall Walk, London SE11 5HJ

2 4 6 8 10 9 7 5 3 1

Text based on the script by Andrew Brenner
Nelly & Nora is created by Gerard O'Rourke and developed by Emma Hogan
Illustrations from the TV animation produced by Geronimo Productions Ltd
Nelly & Nora original artwork and design by Emma Hogan
Licensed by Geronimo Productions Ltd © 2016

This book has been typeset in Baskerville.

Printed in China

British Library Cataloguing in Publication Data:
a catalogue record for this book is available from the British Library

ISBN 978-1-4063-6822-2

www.walker.co.uk

FSC
www.fsc.org
MIX
Paper from
responsible sources
FSC® C101537

# Nelly & Nora

## The Fancy Dress Forest

Nelly

Nora

**WALKER**
ENTERTAINMENT

Squelch squelch
squelch squelch

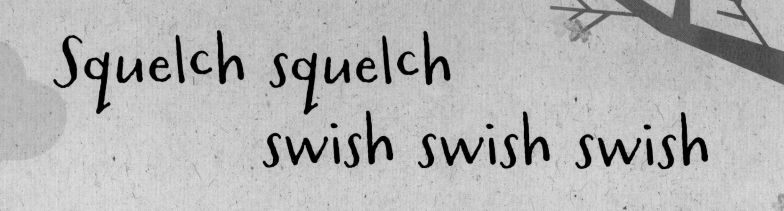

Squelch squelch
swish swish swish

"Look, Nelly!" says Nora.
"All the leaves are falling off the trees."

"It's autumn!"
Nelly says.

"But the trees will get cold without any leaves on,"
says Nora.

"Look!" cries Nelly. "The leaves are sticky!"

She pulls a leaf from her boot. It sticks to her hand instead!

"It's wet," she says, giggling.

"We can stick the leaves
on the trees again!"
says Nelly.

"So the trees will have something to wear to keep them warm!"

Nelly and Nora admire the nicely dressed trees.

"I like the stripy leaves," says Nora.
"They're like stripy pyjamas!"

"This one needs another dark leaf," says Nelly.

"Like this?"

"No, redder."

"Like this one?"

"No, darker...
Like that one over there!"

"Whoaaah!"

When Nora stands up, Nelly giggles.

"You're wearing leaves, too!" says Nelly.

The girls dress up in leaves. It's so much fun!

"We look like autumn trees," giggles Nelly.
"Before the leaves fall off!" laughs Nora.

"Let's show Dad!"

# Squelch squelch squelch

Dad opens the door and calls out,
"Nelly! Nora! Supper's on the
table! Where are you?"

"Surprise, Dad!"

"You look amazing!" he says.
"But I don't think we can bring wet leaves indoors."

"Never mind," says Nora. "We can still be trees, Nelly."

"Trees are still trees when their leaves fall off!" giggles Nelly.
The girls shake and shimmy.

# Make your own fancy-dress leaf crown!

Ask a grown-up to help!

Nelly and Nora made patterns with leaves.
Then they dressed up as trees!
You can, too, in three easy steps.

## YOU WILL NEED:

* A 65 cm x 10 cm sheet of paper or cardboard, something that can bend easily into a round shape

* Craft glue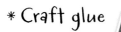

* Tape

* Colourful leaves that have fallen onto the ground. Spend some time outdoors collecting a whole bagful! If no leaves are available, have a grown-up photocopy and cut out the leaf patterns found on the next page, and then colour those in with bright colours.

**1.** First, use pencils, crayons or markers to draw a tree-bark pattern onto the paper and colour it in. This will be the background for the leaves.

**2.** Next, use the glue to stick your leaves onto the drawing, just like Nelly and Nora stuck wet leaves onto the trees in the story. Be sure to mix up the colours! Maybe you can place them in a pattern?

**3.** Ask a grown-up to bend the paper around so that it fits your head. Have them tape the crown together.

Ta-da! **You've created a crown of leaves. Now you can be a tree, too!**